MW01226760

ISAAC ASIMOV'S
Library of the Universe

The Future in Space

by Isaac Asimov and Robert Giraud

Gareth Stevens Publishing
MILWAUKEE

For a free color catalog describing Gareth Stevens' list of high-quality books, call 1-800-341-3569 (USA) or 1-800-461-9120 (Canada)

Library of Congress Cataloging-in-Publication Data

Asimov, Isaac, 1920-
    [l'avenir de la conquête spatiale. English]
    The future in space / by Isaac Asimov and Robert Giraud :
  English text by Patricia Lantier-Sampon. — North American ed.
       p. cm. — (Isaac Asimov's library of the universe)
    Translation of: l'avenir de la conquête spatiale.
    Includes bibliographical references and index.
    Summary: Projects astronomical and astronautical possibilities for the future, such as
huge telescopes, airplanes in space, a probe to the sun, and a landing on Mars.
    ISBN 0-8368-0913-0
    1. Space sciences—Juvenile literature. 2. Astronomy—Juvenile literature. 3.
Astronautics in astronomy—Juvenile literature.
[1. Space sciences. 2. Astronomy. 3. Astronautics.
4. Forecasting.] I. Giraud, Robert, 1921- . II. Title.
III. Series: Asimov, Isaac. 1920-   Library of the universe.
QB500.22.A4513 1993
500.5—dc20   92-34468

North American edition first published in 1993 by
Gareth Stevens Publishing
1555 North RiverCenter Drive, Suite 201
Milwaukee, Wisconsin 53212, USA

U.S. edition ©1993 by Père Castor-Flammarion and Gareth Stevens, Inc.
First published as *l'avenir de la conquête spatiale* © 1992 Père
Castor-Flammarion and Gareth Stevens, Inc. Published by arrangement
with Nightfall, Inc. and Martin H. Greenberg.

Editor: Barbara J. Behm
Technical advisor and consulting editor: Greg Walz-Chojnacki
Translated from the French by Patricia Lantier-Sampon

Printed in the United States of America

1 2 3 4 5 6 7 8 9 97 96 95 94 93

CONTENTS

Introduction 3
Telescopes of Tomorrow 4
New Methods of Investigation 6
A Fleet of Space Shuttles 8
Airplanes in Space 10
Large Space Stations 12
To Better Understand the Sun 14
People on Mars 16
On the Way to Jupiter 18
A Project for Saturn and Its Moon, Titan 20
Europe's Contributions 22
What We Will Know in the Future:
About Our Solar System 24
    . . . and the Universe 26

Calendar of Future Events in Space 28
More Books about the Future of Space Exploration 30
Places to Visit 30
For More Information about the World's Space Programs 30
Glossary 31
Index 32

Nowadays, we have seen all the known planets up close. We have seen dead volcanoes on Mars and live ones on Io, one of Jupiter's moons. We have mapped the surface of Venus and studied the atmosphere of Triton, Neptune's largest moon. We have detected strange objects no one knew anything about until recently: quasars, pulsars, and possible black holes.

Scientists around the world work tirelessly in the endless exploration of space. More advanced space planes and shuttles piloted by experts with a strong spirit of adventure are launched into orbit and beyond each year. Which discoveries, which technical achievements will the human race witness in the years to come? In this book, Isaac Asimov and Robert Giraud guide the reader through the continuous unfolding of the human space adventure.

Telescopes of Tomorrow

For thousands of years, people had no hope of getting a close look at the stars they could see in the sky. It was only with Galileo's telescope in 1609 and Newton's telescope seventy years later that modern astronomy was born. A telescope is an instrument that works because of a mirror, or lens, that gathers and focuses light. The larger the mirror, the better and clearer the image. The largest mirror in a telescope is in the Zelentchouk telescope in the former Soviet Union. This telescope has a 236-inch (6-meter) mirror. It was completed in 1976. A new telescope in Chile will break this record. This telescope is called the VLT (Very Large Telescope), and it will be completed soon. Each of its four mirrors measures 315 inches (8 m). The best of what are known as the multiple-mirror telescopes is the Keck telescope in the Hawaiian Islands. When carefully adjusted, its 36 mirrors of 71 inches (1.8 m) each combine to form a single mirror of 394 inches (10 m). It will soon have a twin, Keck II.

Opposite, top: A quadruple telescope under construction in Chile, as pictured by an artist.

Opposite, bottom: One of the antennae of the VLBA network of radio telescopes located in Arizona.

! Computerized Observation Service
The larger a telescope's mirror or lens, the sharper the view it allows. This is also true of telescopes called radio telescopes. Computers can combine the views from several small radio telescopes into a much sharper one. The VLBA (Very Large Base Array, a network of telescopes with a very large base) is a radio telescope with a unique antenna that spreads out across one-fifth of the Earth's circumference. With a technique called interferometry, these telescopes can identify details on the Moon as close as 3 feet (1 m) apart.

! The Radioscopic Sky
Instead of using mirrors, a radio telescope has an antenna that captures radio waves. A radio telescope can view quasars and galaxies because these bodies emit radio waves. The largest radio telescope antennae are 330 ft. (100 m) in diameter.

5

New Methods of Investigation

The electromagnetic spectrum is made up of a series of adjacent wavelengths. Within this spectrum, the human eye can detect only visible, or ordinary, light. The various rays range from extremely low frequency and long wavelength (at left of diagram) to extremely high frequency and short wavelength (at right of diagram). Electromagnetic waves do not need a medium, such as air, in which to travel. Therefore, they can travel through space to the Earth.

Earth's turbulent atmosphere often blurs the vision of visible light telescopes. A turbulent atmosphere also stops gamma and X-ray radiations, ultraviolet rays, and a large portion of the infrared rays. These rays are all useful in studying births and deaths of stars, supernova explosions, and the mysterious quasars, pulsars, and black holes. To get a clearer view of space, scientists have placed more and more powerful instruments, such as telescopes and satellites, above the Earth's atmosphere.

The Electromagnetic Spectrum

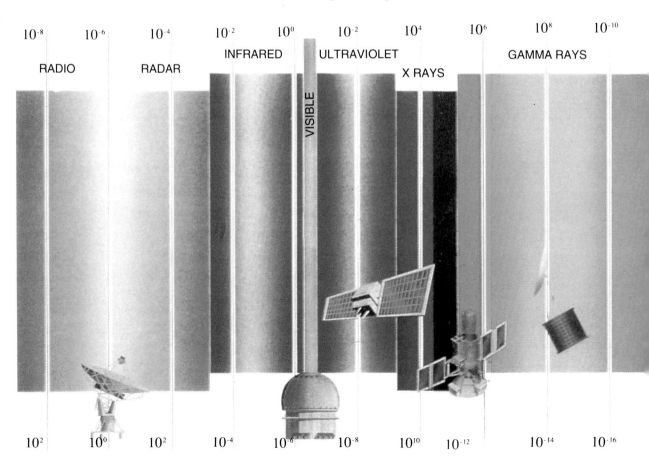

Some of these instruments, classified according to types of radiation, follow.

Visible light: The Hubble Space Telescope (U.S.) was launched in April 1990. It was supposed to expand our ability to study the wonders of space. However, the Hubble has a manufacturer's defect and must be repaired. The European satellite *Hipparcos*, in orbit since 1989, accurately measures the position and movement of 100,000 stars in our galaxy.

Gamma rays: The U.S. satellite *GRO*, launched in April 1991, has already discovered a starlike object called a quasar about seven billion light-years away from Earth. The quasar shines as brilliantly as ten million Milky Ways.

X rays: The international satellite *ROSAT* was placed in orbit in June 1990. So far, it has mapped the locations of more than 100,000 X-ray sources and discovered a number of quasars. It continues to furnish interesting images of several supernovas.

Ultraviolet: The international satellite *IUE* has been in orbit since 1978. It observes interstellar matter and certain galaxies.

Infrared: In 1993, the European satellite *ISO* will begin to study the sources sighted during a sky-scanning project done by the international satellite *IRAS* in 1983.

?

● **What Will Happen to the Hubble Space Telescope?**
The Hubble Space Telescope should be ten times more powerful than any telescope on Earth. Unfortunately, its mirror was manufactured with a slightly imperfect curvature. This keeps it from accomplishing certain missions. In December 1993, a repair team will go into space to fix the Hubble.

An artist's drawing of the satellite *ISO*, complete with its sun visor.

● **A New Way to Launch Rockets**

Rockets fly in space where there is no oxygen. But rocket engines need oxygen in order to work, even for the times they are within the Earth's atmosphere. Airplanes also need oxygen in order for their engines to work. Suppose rockets were launched from airplanes to somehow combine the efforts of both. Would it work? On April 5, 1990, the U.S. rocket Pegasus *was flown to a height of 43,000 feet (13,000 m) by an airplane.* Pegasus *then detached, firing a charge that successfully launched it into orbit.*

A Fleet of Space Shuttles

Unlike the rocket, the shuttle is a reusable spacecraft. It is more expensive than the rocket, but its capabilities are greater. The shuttle can transport seven astronauts as compared to three in a rocket. The shuttle can also recover satellites and small space stations.

Europe has prepared a shuttle for its space station, *Columbus*. The shuttle, *Hermès*, is scheduled to depart in the year 2003 with three persons on board. Unlike the U.S. shuttles that use motors at takeoff assisted by two additional boosters, *Hermès* will be lifted into space on board a rocket. The Japanese are also working on an uninhabited shuttle, similar to *Hermès*, scheduled for takeoff in the year 2000. The future of three shuttles constructed by the former Soviet Union is still uncertain.

Right: U.S. space shuttles land like airplanes.

Opposite, top: Diagram of the European shuttle *Hermès*.

Opposite, bottom: The rocket *Pegasus* at the moment it detaches from its carrier and begins firing its own engines.

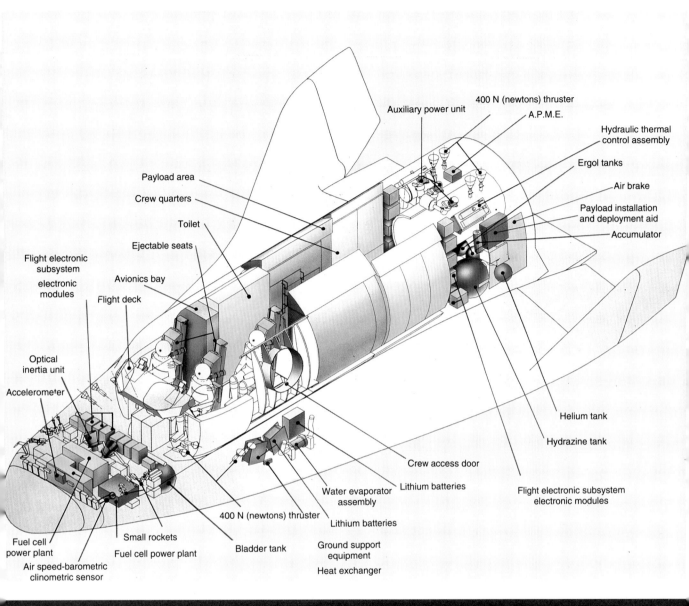

Auxiliary power unit

400 N (newtons) thruster

A.P.M.E.

Hydraulic thermal control assembly

Ergol tanks

Air brake

Payload installation and deployment aid

Accumulator

Payload area

Crew quarters

Toilet

Ejectable seats

Flight electronic subsystem electronic modules

Avionics bay

Flight deck

Optical inertia unit

Accelerometer

Fuel cell power plant

Air speed-barometric clinometric sensor

Small rockets

Fuel cell power plant

400 N (newtons) thruster

Bladder tank

Water evaporator assembly

Lithium batteries

Ground support equipment

Heat exchanger

Lithium batteries

Crew access door

Helium tank

Hydrazine tank

Flight electronic subsystem electronic modules

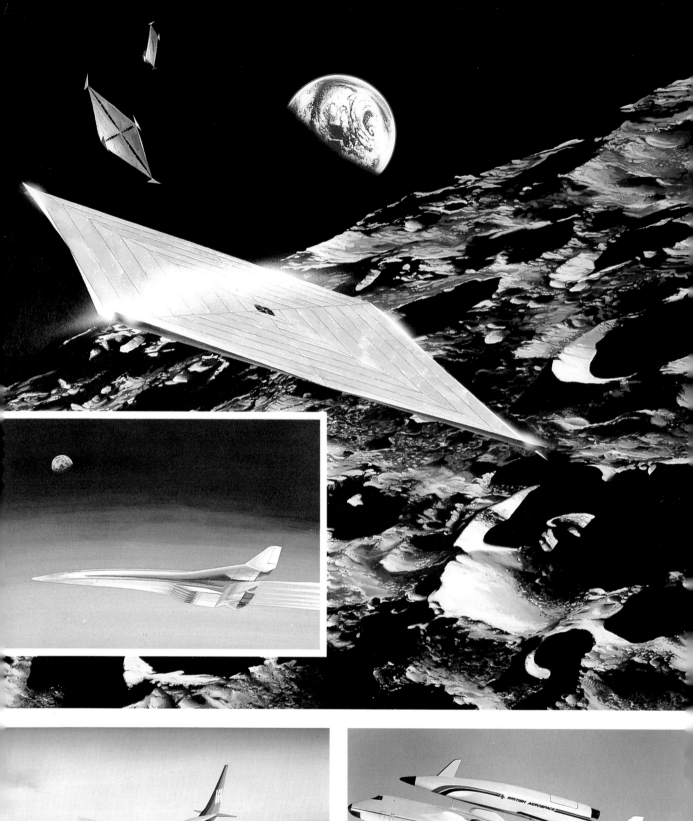

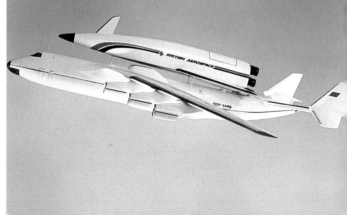

Airplanes in Space

The traditional rocket, the space fleet, and airborne rockets may someday be replaced by an airplane called the transatmospheric airplane. This airplane could thrust itself into space from a horizontal takeoff position. To do this, it would use oxygen from the air until it reaches the highest altitude possible, about 15 miles (25 km). After that, it would use oxygen stored in its tanks.

In 1986, the United States began work on the *NASP*, or *X30*, an experimental aircraft designed to fly at the high speed necessary to reach outer space. France is working on the *AGV*, or *Avion à Grande Vitesse* (Airplane of Great Speed). This vehicle will be able to transport 150 passengers at a speed of more than 3,100 miles per hour (5,000 km/hr) to an altitude of 19 miles (30 km). The German *Sänger* project and the British *HOTOL* project will result in airplanes that are able to reach orbit. These planes will fly through the air at high speed until they enter outer space. They will return to the ground like ordinary airplanes. They are being designed to carry passengers and cargo.

Opposite, inset: What a future U.S. hypersonic, or high-speed, airplane might look like.

Opposite, top: An immense sail, unfurled in space, travels toward its destination.

Opposite, bottom left: Sketch of the French project *AGV*, or Avion à Grande Vitesse (Airplane of Great Speed).

Opposite, bottom right: Britain's space airplane, *HOTOL*, is seen traveling on top of its huge transporter, *Autonov-225*.

● **Mariner 10** *and a Mission to the Moon*
Mariner *refers to a series of U.S. space probes that has provided information about Mercury, Venus, and Mars.* Mariner 10 *was launched in 1973. Due to the probe's many accomplishments, scientists from the United States, Europe, and Japan are organizing a joint mission to the Moon. Hopefully, this mission will be underway by 1994.*

● *Propulsion in Outer Space*
Different types of propulsion are available for use in outer space. Rocket chemical engines are powered by the reaction of fuel and oxygen. Ionic engines can attain considerable speed but are not very powerful. Nuclear energy in the form of nuclearthermics is also available. However, this type of propulsion has been found to be a potential danger to the environment.

Large Space Stations

Scientists conduct many types of experiments to gather information about outer space. For example, experts must test the ability of the human body to withstand interplanetary flights lasting several years before such flights actually take place. Tests of this type need to be conducted at space stations. But space stations are too expensive for any one country alone to operate. Therefore, several countries are combining their efforts to operate a space station. *Freedom* is a large international space station project composed of several independent units or modules (one U.S., one European, and one Japanese). These modules will connect with each other in space. In 1992, Europe launched a space platform called *Eureka* into orbit as part of the preparations for the project, *Columbus*.

A drawing of the orbital unit Columbus *at the space station* Freedom.

! The Biosphere 2 Experiment

In October 1991, four men and four women enclosed themselves for a two-year period in a world under glass. The experimental project is called Biosphere 2. The occupants are operating a simulated space colony, growing their own food and recycling air, water, and waste. Biosphere 2 covers an area of three acres and is located in Oracle, Arizona, 35 miles north of Tucson in the United States. The project has its supporters and its critics. An outside panel of scientists will review the credibility of Biosphere 2. And, of course, history will be the final judge of Biosphere 2's contributions to science.

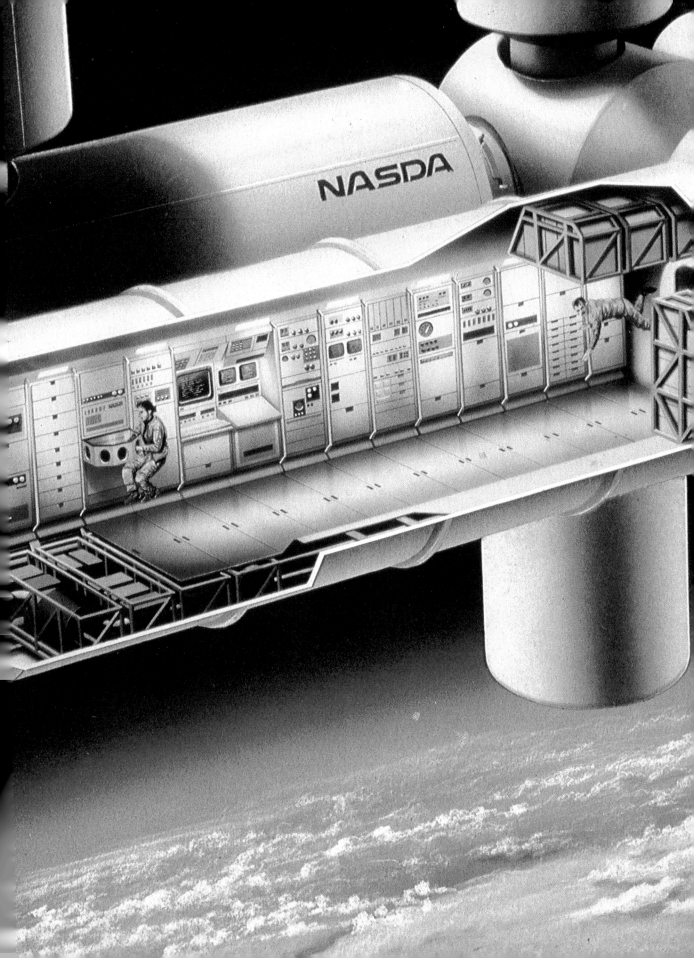

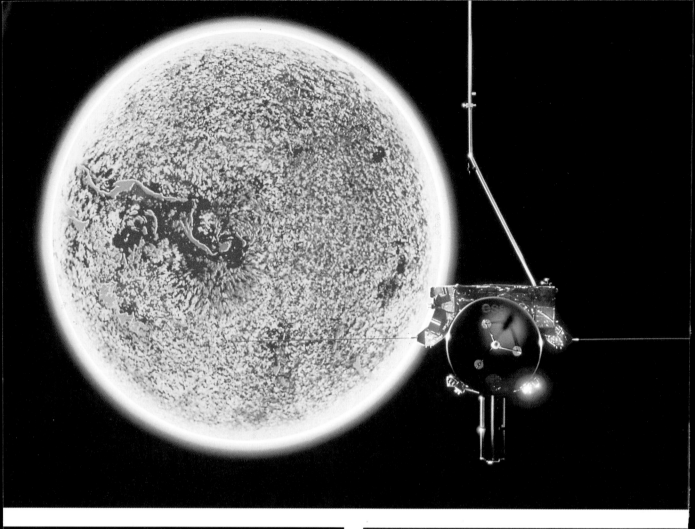

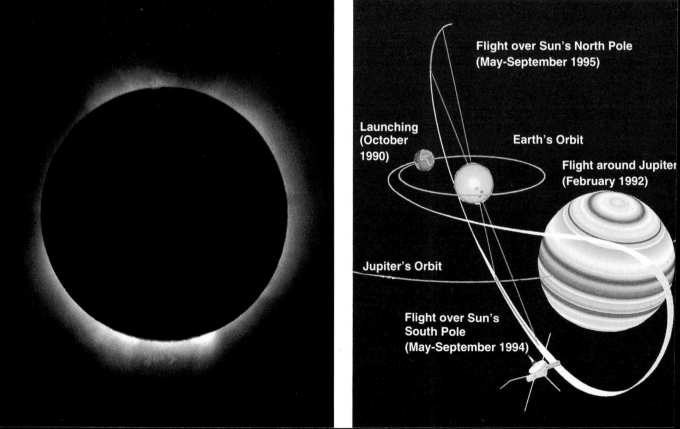

Flight over Sun's North Pole
(May-September 1995)

Launching
(October
1990)

Earth's Orbit

Flight around Jupiter
(February 1992)

Jupiter's Orbit

Flight over Sun's
South Pole
(May-September 1994)

To Better Understand the Sun

The Sun is the only star that may be within our reach. As on other stars, violent and abundant phenomena occur on the Sun's surface. These phenomena, for the most part, have nothing in common with the types of activity that occur on the Earth's surface.

The European space probe *Ulysses*, launched in October 1990, will be the first probe to fly over the poles of the Sun. Matter and radiation are less affected by the rotation and magnetic field of the Sun at the poles.

The European Space Agency (ESA) plans to place the probe *Soho* in orbit in 1995. *Soho* will be an orbital observatory equipped to study the sun. It will carry scientific instruments such as spectrometers, telescopes, and a coronograph. *Soho* will also have the ability to detect small oscillations of solar matter, in which the photosphere, or the part of the Sun we see, "rings" like a bell.

● *The Solar Eclipse of July 11, 1991*
The part of the Sun we can see is the photosphere. Above the photosphere are the fainter chromosphere and corona. These outer layers are usually lost in the brilliant glow of the photosphere. During what is known as a total solar eclipse, the moon completely covers the photosphere. This makes it possible to see the outer regions of the Sun's atmosphere. On July 11, 1991, one of the world's best-equipped observatories, located at Mauna Kea in Hawaii, found itself in the shady zone of the Moon. Total solar eclipses occur only once or twice a year somewhere on Earth. Several hundred years pass between eclipses at the same location.

Opposite, top: The *Ulysses* probe.

Opposite, left: The blazing streamers in the solar corona are visible during total solar eclipses like the one that occurred on July 11, 1991.

Opposite, right: The gravity on Jupiter propelled the probe *Ulysses* in a course perpendicular to the orbits of the planets at a speed of 282,116 miles per hour (454,000 km/hr). This is the fastest speed ever attained in a human-built spacecraft.

15

People on Mars

Mars has fascinated people for a long time. Exploring this planet promises to be the great space event of the first part of the twenty-first century. The United States has made many plans detailing its possible journeys to Mars. The program officially began in 1992 with the U.S. launch of the Mars *Observer* probe. The *Observer* will make detailed maps of potential landing sites. The Russians will launch a probe toward Mars in 1994 that will carry two French balloon probes for atmospheric studies. In 1996, Russia will launch another probe loaded with mobile surface engines. The program includes a ten-year study of the climate and soil of Mars. The first astronauts should arrive on Mars by 2016. In addition to the Mars projects, voyages to the Moon should resume around 2003-2005. These have been abandoned since 1972. The Moon will rapidly become the main base of departure for interplanetary flights.

Opposite, top: The second celestial body people will walk on is Mars. The first was the Moon.

Opposite, bottom left: Scientists will observe Mars from their position on Phobos, a moon of Mars.

Opposite, bottom right: The Russian vehicle that will travel to Mars is capable of carrying a load of 110-220 pounds (50-100 kg). It will land on Mars in 1996.

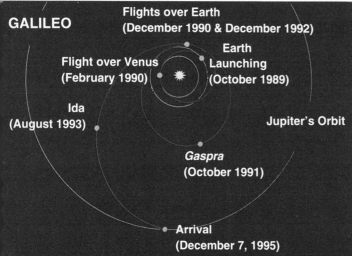

GALILEO

Flights over Earth
(December 1990 & December 1992)

Flight over Venus
(February 1990)

Earth
Launching
(October 1989)

Ida
(August 1993)

Jupiter's Orbit

Gaspra
(October 1991)

Arrival
(December 7, 1995)

On the Way to Jupiter

Launched in October 1989, the U.S. space probe *Galileo* has so far brushed near Venus in February 1990 and Earth in December 1990. It is scheduled to pass close to Earth again in December 1992. On October 29, 1991, at a distance of only 995 miles (1,600 km) away, it began the first survey of an asteroid ever performed by a probe. If there is no change in the program, *Galileo* will reach Jupiter in December 1995. Its orbiter will circle the giant planet for twenty months. Another probe will then be released into the depths of Jupiter's atmosphere. This probe should be able to take measurements for at least one hour before being destroyed by the high temperature and pressure that exist in the depths of Jupiter's atmosphere.

? How Can *Galileo* Be Fixed?

Galileo's main antenna failed to open as planned shortly after launch. This antenna is needed in order to send pictures and data back to Earth from Jupiter. NASA's engineers have experience fixing spacecraft that are millions of miles from Earth. One way to open the antenna is to turn the craft back and forth, hoping the change from cold to hot (caused by sunlight) will loosen the antenna. Another plan is to quickly start and stop the antenna motor to "hammer" the antenna open. *Galileo* has a small antenna that still works, but it is weaker than the main antenna and can send only a tiny amount of information from Jupiter.

Top: The probe *Galileo*, placed by an artist on a photo of Jupiter.

Opposite, far left: Unlike on Earth, a straight line in space is not the shortest route between points.
Opposite, left: The first close-up of an asteroid, *Gaspra, as seen by Galileo* in 1991.

A Project for Saturn and Its Moon, Titan

The launching of the U.S. probe *Cassini* in 1995 or 1997 should begin one of the most exciting stages of the exploration of the Solar System. *Cassini* is an advanced space probe that will become an artificial satellite of the planet Saturn in 2005. On board will be the European probe *Huygens* that will aim toward the surface of Titan, a moon of Saturn. *Cassini* will circle Saturn at its ring system for four years. It will study in detail Saturn's atmosphere, its rings, and its magnetosphere (the zone influenced by its magnetic field). *Huygens* will analyze, in the course of its descent, the atmosphere of Titan and send the information back to Earth. It will then either crash or sink into Titan's surface, depending on whether the surface is solid or liquid.

Inset, right: The route that *Cassini* will follow to reach Saturn.

Right: The predicted flight of *Cassini* and its module *Huygens* after their separation on the outskirts of Saturn.

❗ ● *The Mysteries of Titan*

Titan is the ninth-largest body in the Solar System. Unlike all the other moons, it has a thick atmosphere. The probe Voyager *has located some organic compounds in Titan's atmosphere. Under certain conditions, the types of compounds that were found can generate living matter. Titan's surface, hidden by the thickness of its atmosphere, remains a puzzle. It is possible that it might be entirely or partially covered by an ocean of methane gas.* Huygens *will reveal the answer.*

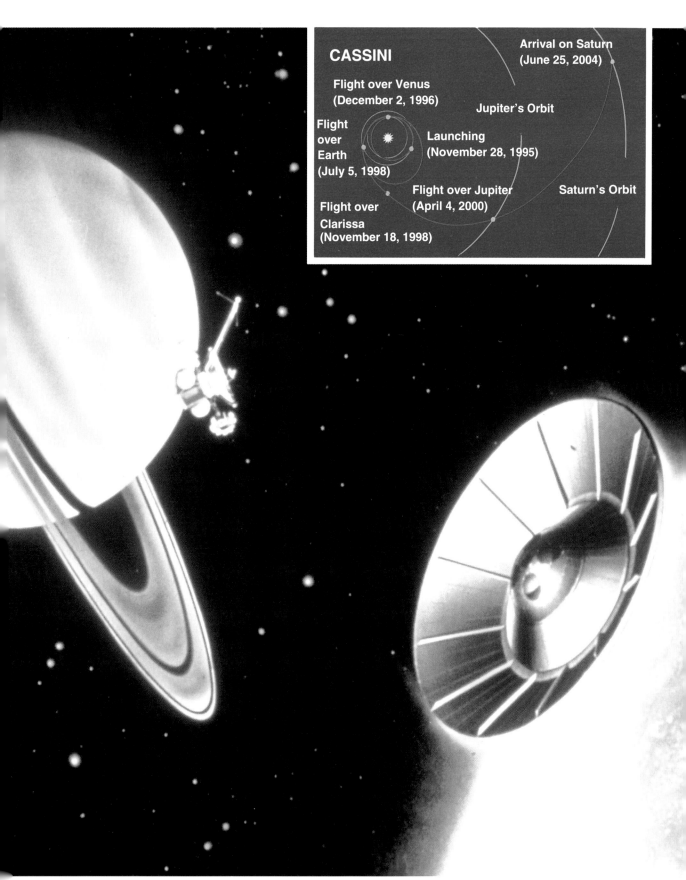

CASSINI

Flight over Venus
(December 2, 1996)

Arrival on Saturn
(June 25, 2004)

Jupiter's Orbit

Flight
over
Earth
(July 5, 1998)

Launching
(November 28, 1995)

Flight over Jupiter
(April 4, 2000)

Saturn's Orbit

Flight over
Clarissa
(November 18, 1998)

ERS-1

ariane

cnes

V 44

Europe's Contributions

The European Space Agency (ESA) was created in 1975. Member countries of the organization include Germany, Austria, Belgium, Denmark, Spain, France, Ireland, Italy, Norway, the Netherlands, the United Kingdom, Sweden, and Switzerland. Finland is scheduled to join in 1995.

The ESA has built the booster *Ariane*, which will launch most civilian satellites. It has already successfully launched telecommunications, meteorological, and teledetection (for the study of terrestrial surfaces) satellites.

As a part of its program, the ESA is forming a corps of astronauts around Germany's Ulf Merbold, the Netherlands' Wubbo Ockers (both of whom have already participated in the ESA's and NASA's *Spacelab* missions), Belgium's Dirk Frimout, and Switzerland's Claude Nicollier. Only six astronauts were in the program in 1991, but the ESA hopes to recruit thirty astronauts by the end of the century.

!

● ***In Limbo***
Russian cosmonaut Sergei Krikalev began his mission in space on May 18, 1991, orbiting the Earth in the space station Mir. He was to return home after just five months. During his third month in space, however, a coup was attempted in his country to preserve the communist government. The coup failed, and the former Soviet Union's space program was put on hold for financial reasons. This meant that Krikalev had to stay in space indefinitely. A rocket containing food and supplies was launched to him. Eventually, after 313 days in space, Krikalev was allowed to return to Earth—and to a country with an uncertain future.

Opposite: The European booster *Ariane* at the moment of firing.

Left: Because of the break-up of the former Soviet Union, the long-range future of space station *Mir* is unknown. A crew is pictured on board *Mir* in 1988.

What We Will Know in the Future: about Our Solar System . . .

Our Ancestors, Interstellar Space?
Scientists are not certain that the water and organic substances necessary for life on Earth could have formed entirely on Earth. In fact, these elements also appear in space among the stars and on the comets. Each year, several hundred tons of space debris fall in small pieces toward Earth. This bombardment was much more intense during the early years of Earth's history. In time, the role of asteroids and comets at the beginning of life on Earth will become clearer thanks to a close study of samplings of asteroids and comets.

The Search for Signs of Life
Humans have not yet discovered biological activity on any of the other planets, not even primitive life. Perhaps someday, however, we will succeed in locating signs of life on Mars, on Titan, or in the deep layers of atmosphere on another planet.

A Hurricane on Saturn
Since September 1990, scientists have observed (thanks to the Hubble) a hurricane on Saturn. Its winds blow at 995 miles per hour (1,600 km/hr). This is about five or six times stronger than the most devastating hurricane on Earth. The Great Red Spot of Jupiter and the Great Dark Spot of Neptune are also atmospheric disturbances. *Galileo* and *Cassini* will help explain some of these occurrences on the planets.

!

● *Mines . . . of Information*
Asteroids and comets have changed little since their formation. Therefore, they can furnish valuable information about the beginnings of our Solar System. Asteroids and comets may even hold the key to the appearance of life on Earth and the disappearance of the dinosaurs. In the course of their voyages, the probes Galileo *and* Cassini *have or will come close to several asteroids. The European probe* Giotto, *which approached Halley's Comet in 1986, also passed within 620 miles (1,000 km) of the comet Grigg-Skjellerup. The Rosetta mission, sponsored by the ESA, plans to bring back samples of matter from a comet.*

The Dinosaurs, Victims of the Comets?

Scientists are studying a giant crater, parts of which were discovered recently in the Yucatan in Mexico. The scientists want to find out if the crater was hollowed out 65 million years ago by the fall of an enormous celestial body. Such an occurrence would have thrown vast quantities of debris and dust into the atmosphere. This would have greatly changed the climate, perhaps leading to the disappearance of the dinosaurs and three-quarters of the other animal species on Earth.

Below, left: The fall of a large celestial body could have altered Earth's climate, causing the disappearance of the dinosaurs.

Below, right top: Titan's thick fog covers many mysteries.

Below, right bottom: Turbulent formations on Saturn's surface.

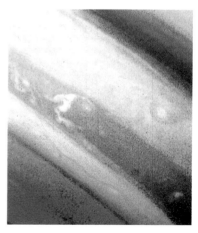

. . . and the Universe

Scientists have found evidence that distant galaxies are rushing away from Earth at a higher speed than closer galaxies. In fact, the speed of the galaxies seems to be directly connected to their distances from Earth. This connection is one of the reasons most scientists accept the Big Bang theory of the formation of the universe. According to this theory, the universe began with a huge explosion that created a smooth, even "soup" of matter and energy. This "soup" became lumpy as stars, planets, and galaxies formed. Astronomers are currently trying to discover why these developments might have taken place.

Bottomless Pits of the Universe
The huge assortment of instruments that scientists use to study space constantly uncovers new information that may help prove the existence of black holes, areas in space with intensely strong gravitational fields. In 1991, scientists discovered, about 300 million light-years from Earth, signs pointing toward the existence of what might be the most gigantic of all the black holes.

Clues to the Mysteries
The centers of galaxies seem to behave as though they are under the influence of masses of undetectable matter. Also, the velocity of stars at the heart of the galaxies does not seem to have a satisfactory explanation. The study of certain objects in space, such as cosmic dusts and black holes, may clear up these mysteries.

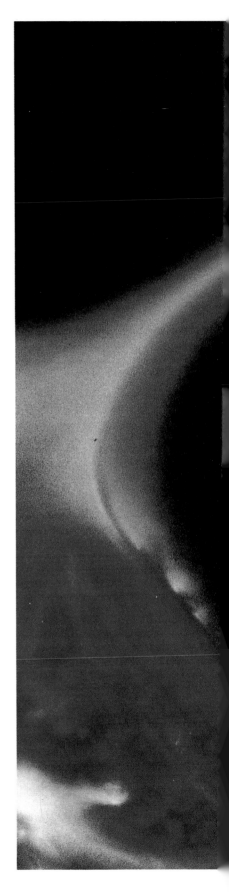

Distant Counterparts of Earth

If extraterrestrial life forms do exist, they could only survive on planets. Innumerable planets probably exist in the Universe, but they are so faint in brightness when compared to the stars that they are difficult to detect and observe. Thanks to infrared telescopes, scientists have already located disks around stars. Planets may be forming – or already exist – in these disks. With the combined efforts of the satellite *ISO*, the Hubble Space Telescope, and networks of terrestrial telescopes, extrasolar planets may be discovered very soon.

Opposite: Although scientists are not certain if black holes really exist, a black hole is imagined as having a strong gravitational pull.

Left: The day when Earthlings will be able to fly over a distant planet is still far in the future.

Calendar of Future Events in Space: 1990s and Beyond

1993

May:
Launching of the European infrared observatory *ISO.*

June:
Recovery of the European platform *Eureka,* which was placed in orbit in August 1992 by the Swiss astronaut Claude Nicollier from the shuttle *Atlantis.* This platform will leave again for a new flight in 1994.

August:
Galileo scheduled to fly past the asteroid Ida.

December:
Service to the Hubble Space Telescope by a U.S. shuttle.

1994

March:
Departure of the Russian mission to Mars.

May to September:
Ulysses will fly over and survey the Sun's south pole.

1995

NASA will launch pressurized modules for the international space station *Freedom.*

The first mirror of the huge telescope VLT in Chile will be put into service.

Firing of the European booster *Ariane 5,* designed to place 20 tons in a low orbit and 7 tons in geostationary orbit. It will also launch the shuttle *Hermès.*

May to September:
Ulysses will fly over and survey the north pole of the Sun.

June:
Launching of the U.S. satellite *SWAS* for the study of millimetric waves.

July:
Launching of *Soho* (ESA).

December:
Launching of the European satellite *Cluster* to study the impact of the Sun on the particles and the magnetic field surrounding Earth.

Arrival of *Galileo* in the atmosphere of Jupiter.

1996

Departure of the second Russian mission to Mars.

Completion of the Keck II telescope in the Hawaiian Islands (United States).

1997

October:
Launching of *Cassini.*

1998

Launching of the European X-ray observatory X XMM (ESA).

Permanent occupation of the space station *Freedom,* including the habitable *Columbus* module.

1999

Launching of the American X-ray observatory AXAF.

1999-2000

Satellite reconnaissance envoy prepares for the U.S. arrival on the Moon.

2000

Cassini flies over and surveys Jupiter.

Completion of the large telescope VLT with its four mirrors of 315 inches (8 m) each. It will have the equivalent of a single 53-foot (16-m) mirror, the largest and most powerful ever used by astronomers.

2001

Period of maximum solar activity, after the one of 1990 (11-year cycles).

Departure toward Mars of the first of the four American mini-laboratories *Mesur.* The second will follow in 2002, and the two final ones will depart in 2005.

2002

The probe *Huygens* (*Cassini* mission) should descend toward Titan.

Launching of the Rosetta mission.

2003

The European shuttle *Hermès* will carry its first three astronauts.

The independent module of the European space station *Columbus* will perform its first mission.

Between 2003 and 2005

NASA anticipates the installation of an automatic experimental factory for the exploration of lunar resources, then the launching of six astronauts who will spend fourteen days on the Moon.

2008

Arrival of Rosetta on a comet to gather samples.

2010

Following the appraisals of NASA, the installation of twelve people on the Moon.

2012 and 2014

According to NASA's plans, the unloading of necessary supplies on Mars.

2016

The most probable date, after NASA's calculations, for the Mars landing.

in 20,000 years

The probes *Voyager 1* and *Voyager 2* (launched in 1977) will travel across the Oort Cloud located at the extreme limits of the Solar System.

in 40,000 years

Voyager 1 will pass within 1.6 light-years of a star in the giraffe constellation Camelopardalis, about three light-years away from Earth.

in 296,000 years

Voyager 2 will find itself in the distant suburbs of Sirius, the brightest star in the heavens, 8.6 light-years away from Earth.

More Books about the Future of Space Exploration

Here are more books about the future in space. Check your local library or bookstore to see if they have them or can order them for you.

Distance Flights. Berliner (Lerner)
The Enterprise and Beyond. Halprin (Halprin)
Journey to the Outer Planets. Barker (Rourke)
The NOVA Space Explorer's Guide: Where to Go and What to See. Maurer (Clarkson N. Potter)
Passage to Space: The Shuttle Transport System. Coombs (William Morrow)
Space Exploration and Travel. Sabin (Troll Associates)
Space Station. Apfel (Franklin Watts)
Space Travel. A Technological Frontier. DeOld and Judge (Davis Mass)

Places to Visit

Here are some centers and museums with exhibits and information about future space exploration and travel.

The Smithsonian
   Institution
Washington, D.C.

International Women's Air
   and Space Museum
Centerville, Ohio

National Air and Space
   Museum
Washington, D.C.

Edmonton Space Sciences
   Centre
Edmonton, Alberta

Palomar Observatory
Palomar Mountain, California

The Museum of Science and
   Industry
Chicago, Illinois

For More Information about the World's Space Programs . . .

For more information about space programs, write to the following organizations. Be sure to tell them exactly what you want to know about, and include your full name and address so they can write back to you.

For information about the U.S. space program:
NASA Kennedy Space Center
Educational Services Office
Kennedy Space Center,
   Florida 32899

NASA Jet Propulsion Laboratory
4800 Oak Grove Drive
Pasadena, California 91109

For information about the Canadian space program:
Space Resources Centre
Marc Garneau Collegiate Institute
135 Overlea Boulevard
Don Mills, Ontario M3C 1B3

For information about the European space program:
European Space Agency
Washington Office
955 L'Enfant Plaza SW
Suite 1404
Washington, D.C. 20024

For more information about the Russian space program:
Glavcosmos, Russia
9 Krasnoproletarskay VI
103030 Moscow, Russia

Glossary

asteroid: A very small planet, made of rock or metal, of which there are thousands in our Solar System. Most can be found orbiting the Sun between Mars and Jupiter in a "belt" formation.

atmosphere: The gaseous mass that surrounds a planet, moon, or star.

black hole: A hypothetical object in space thought to be formed by the explosion and collapse of a star. The object is so dense that even light cannot escape the incredible force of its gravity.

booster: A solid fuel rocket used to help space vehicles lift off. A booster is also referred to as a solid rocket.

galaxy: A very large grouping of celestial bodies. Our Solar System is just one part of a vast galaxy.

infrared ray: A ray with a wavelength that is just beyond the red end of the visible spectrum of light. Infrared rays are used to obtain pictures of objects in space that are obscured by haze in the atmosphere. Visible light is scattered by haze, but infrared rays are not.

magnetosphere: The zone surrounding a planet that is influenced by its magnetic field.

meteor: A chunk of matter from space that enters Earth's atmosphere and usually quickly burns up.

NASA: The abbreviation for the National Aeronautics and Space Administration, the United States government agency that plans and operates space flights and exploration.

neutrino: A tiny particle produced when hydrogen fuses to helium in the center of the Sun.

observatory: A building or other structure designed for observing and recording celestial movements and events.

orbit: The path that an object follows around a planet or star. An object can remain in orbit without relying on engine power because the force of gravity pulls it toward the planet or star.

photosphere: The luminous surface layer of the Sun or another star.

probe: A spacecraft that photographs celestial bodies as they travel through space. Sometimes probes also land on these bodies.

pulsar: A cosmic source, such as a star, of regularly and rapidly pulsating radio signals.

quasar: A very distant and very luminous object found at the center of a galaxy.

satellite: An object that orbits another object in space. A moon is a natural satellite, while weather satellites or communications satellites built to orbit Earth are referred to as artificial.

shuttle: A "recyclable" spacecraft that allows for the recovery of satellites and small space stations.

space station: A well-equipped laboratory that allows scientists to live and carry out research over longer periods of time in space. At present, such stations have proven too costly to support life for more than short periods of time.

spectrometer: An instrument that measures the wavelengths of images formed by rays of light or other radiation or sound.

telescope: An instrument that uses an arrangement of mirrors or lenses in a long tube to make objects that are far away appear to be closer.

ultraviolet ray: A ray with a wavelength just beyond the violet end of the visible spectrum of light. The sun produces a large amount of ultraviolet light, but most of it is absorbed in the ozone layer, an area in the upper atmosphere of the Earth.

Index

AGV 11
Ariane 23
Asteroids 19, 24

Biosphere 2 12
Black holes 6, 26, 27

Cassini 20, 21, 24
Chromosphere 15
Columbus 8, 12
Comets 24, 25
Corona 15
Cosmic dusts 26
Cosmonaut 23

Dinosaurs 24, 25

Electromagnetic spectrum 6
Eureka 12
European Space Agency 15,
    23, 24
Extrasolar planets 27
Extraterrestrial life 27

Freedom 12

Galaxies 5, 26
Galileo 5
Galileo 18, 19, 24
Gamma rays 7
Gaspra 18, 19
Giotto 24
Great Dark Spot 24
Great Red Spot 24
Grigg-Skjellerup 24
GRO 7

Halley's Comet 24
Hermès 8
Hipparcos 7

HOTOL 11
Hubble Space Telescope 7,
    24, 27
Huygens 20

Infrared rays 6, 7
Interferometry 5
Interstellar matter 5, 24
Interstellar space 24
Ionic engine 11
ISO 7, 27
IUE 7

Jupiter 14, 15, 18, 19, 21

Keck telescope 5
Krikalev, Sergei 23

Lens 5

Mariner 10 11
Mars 11, 16, 17, 24
Methane gas 20
Mexico, Yucatan 25
Milky Way 5, 7
Mir 23
Mirror 5, 7

NASA 19
NASP 11
Neptune 24
Newton 5

Observer 16

Pegasus 8
Phobos 16
Photosphere 15

Quasars 5, 6, 7

Radio waves 5
Rockets 8, 9

Sänger 11
Satellites 7, 8
Saturn 20, 21, 24, 25
Shuttle 8
Soho 15
Solar corona 15
Solar eclipse 15
Solar System 20, 24
Soviet Union, former 5, 8, 23
Space probe 11, 15, 16,
    20, 21
Space stations 8, 12
Spacelab 23
Stars 6, 15, 26
Sun 15
Supernovas 6, 7

Telescopes 5, 6, 27
Titan 20, 24, 25
Transatmospheric airplane 11

Ultraviolet rays 6, 7
Ulysses 15

Visible light 7
VLBA 5
VLT 5
Voyager 20

Wavelength 6

X rays 6, 7
X30 11

Zelentchouk 5

The publishers wish to thank the following for permission to reproduce copyright material: cover, p. 7, p. 10 (lower right), pp. 12-13, p. 14 (upper), © European Space Agency (ESA); p. 4 (upper), p. 16 (upper), © L. Bret/Ciel et Espace; p. 4 (lower), p. 14 (lower left), © S. Brunier/Ciel et Espace; p. 6, CNES; p. 8, p. 9 (lower), p. 10 (center), pp. 18-19, 20-21, © NASA/Ciel et Espace; p. 9 (upper), Aérospatiale/ESA; p. 10 (upper), © Manchu/Ciel et Espace; p. 10 (lower left), Aérospatiale; p. 14 (lower right), dessin ESA/Ciel et Espace; pp. 16-17, © D. Hardy/Ciel et Espace; p. 16 (lower), IKI/ Ciel et Espace; p. 18 (left), p. 21, Ciel et Espace; p. 18 (right), © JPL/Ciel et Espace; p. 22, ESA/CNES; p. 23, CNES/ Glavcosmos; p. 25 (left), © Julian Baum; p. 25 (upper right), © Paul Dimare, 1988; p. 25 (lower right), Jet Propulsion Laboratory; pp. 26-27, © Mark Paternostro, 1988; p. 27, © Doug McLeod, 1988.